STICKER BOOK

ISBN 978-0-545-31214-1

12 11 10 9 8 7 6 5 4 3 2 1 11 12 13 14 15 16/0

Printed in Malaysia 106 First printing, June 2011

SCHOLASTIC INC.
NEW YORK TORONTO LONDON AUCKLAND
SYDNEY MEXICO CITY NEW DELHI HONG KONG

Witches and wizards buy wands, school supplies, and magical books from the shops in Diagon Alley.

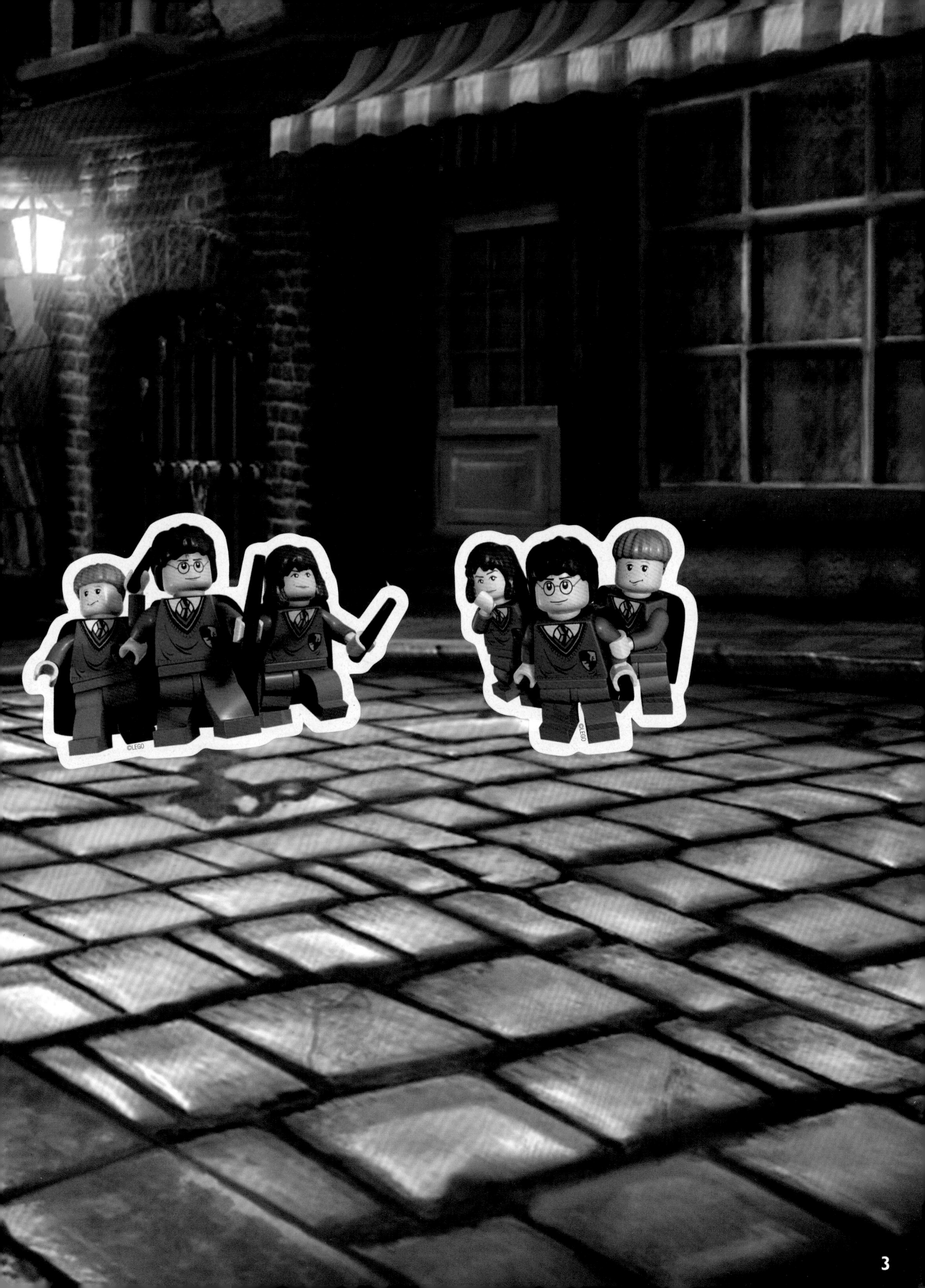
©LEGO
©LEGO

Students and professors walk through the hallways of Hogwarts.

Harry is the Seeker for the Gryffindor Quidditch team. The Gryffindor Quidditch team plays against the other houses on the Quidditch pitch.

LEGO
Harry Potter

USE THESE STICKERS ON PAGES 2-3
©LEGO
©LEGO
©LEGO
©LEGO
©LEGO
USE THESE STICKERS
ON PAGES 4-5
©LEGO
©LEGO
©LEGO
©LEGO
©LEGO
©LEGO

USE THESE STICKERS ON PAGES 6-7

USE THESE STICKERS ON PAGES 8-9

USE THESE STICKERS
ANYWHERE YOU WANT!

USE THESE STICKERS ON PAGES 10-11

USE THESE STICKERS ANYWHERE YOU WANT!

USE THESE STICKERS
ON PAGE 12
USE THESE STICKERS
ANYWHERE YOU WANT!

LEGO
Harry Potter

The tunnel to the Chamber of Secrets is very dark.

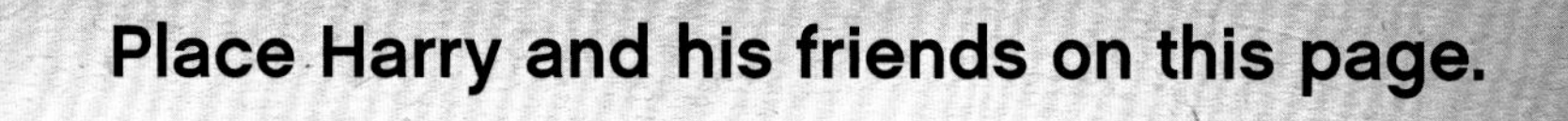
Place Harry and his friends on this page.

HARRY POTTER™

RON WEASLEY™

HERMIONE GRANGER™

ALBUS DUMBLEDORE™

NEVILLE LONGBOTTOM™
GEORGE WEASLEY
FRED WEASLEY
RUBEUS HAGRID™
SIRIUS BLACK™

Place Voldemort and his followers on this page.
LORD VOLDEMORT™
QUIRINUS QUIRRELL
DEATH EATER
Place the Dursley family here.
VERNON DURSLEY
DUDLEY DURSLEY™
PETUNIA DURSLEY